My little one, lay down your head.
It's time to doze, it's time for bed.

You tell me, "I'm not sleepy now."
"Just try," I say. You ask me, "*How?*"

The answer, darling little child,
is every creature, tame and wild,
has *night* and *day*, has *still* and *leap*,
has *wide awake* and *sound asleep*.

Look! Even all the awake
animals are getting sleepy.

In fact...

Antelope is already asleep,
all the way to his antlers.

Baby Bison has bedded
down beside her brother,
by the barn.

Cat's curled up on
a crimson couch cushion,

while Chimpanzee's created
a cozy cradle of leaves,
and she and her child
climb in, cuddling.

After a day in the desert, Dromedary drops down to his knees, dozing under the date palms.

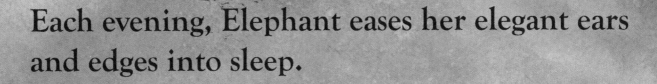

Each evening, Elephant eases her elegant ears
and edges into sleep.

Fox, fading fast,
finds rest in the forest,

while Frog just floats, letting her feet flop
until they find firm footing near the ferns.

Goose and Gander say,
"Good night, darling goslings,"
and they all go to sleep in the garden.

Hedgehog is hibernating,
hiding in her hole.

Ibex inches
his way up
the icy incline
toward a good
day's nap.

And Jaguar stops jumping
through the jungle, just resting now.

Kangaroo and
Koala are kin:

each curls up in his
mother's king-sized,
kid-sized pouch.

As the light laps the leaves, Lion lies down, lounging low with Lioness and the little ones.

Mole makes a
mattress of mud
as the moon rises
over the mountain,

while Nightingale naps
in a nest near the ground.

Otter, overcome,
is out in the ocean,
rocking on and on
oh-so-gently.

In a protected place on a precipice,
Panda plumps down peacefully.

Quetzal, wrapped in her quilt
of feathers, grows quiet.

Rabbit relaxes into restful repose,
dreaming of ripe red radishes.

Swan, eyes shut, slumbers,
standing single-legged on
the shore

as Snake sighs, and starts to slither
toward a sweet, slumberous snooze...

and Sloth
just
sleeps.

Turtle's tired, and turns in,
tucking each tiny toe
into her tight shell.

Underneath an umbrella of leaves,
Urubu nestles his head under his night-black wing,
unaware of the waking world.

Vole vanishes into a
violet-shadowed valley.

Walrus wades into the waves and catches forty wet winks.

Expecting an exceptionally
excellent
night's rest,

Yak yawns,

and Zebra just Zzzzzzzzzzs.

An alphabet of ways to sleep,
of ways to rest and ways to keep
a stillness, quiet through the dark,
without a chirp or roar or bark.

Each animal, from A to Z,
has found itself so sleepily
its pond or tree or pile of hay
to rest in, nest in, Z to A.

And you, my little human one?
Since night is here and day is done,
and since you have a cozy bed,
a pillow for your dozy head,
with no more *why* and not one *how*
might you, like them, start sleeping now?

Ssssh...

sssssh...

sssssshhh.